Visit us on the Web!
randomhousekids.com
SesameStreetBooks.com
www.sesamestreet.org

For more information and resources, visit sesamestreet.org/autism

Educators and librarians, for a variety of teaching tools, visit us at RHTeachersLibrarians.com

ISBN 978-1-5247-6621-4

Printed in the United States of America
10 9 8 7 6 5 4 3 2 1

Major support for this initiative provided by American Greetings. Generous support provided by the Robert R. McCormick Foundation and Kristen Rohr.

123 SESAME STREET

We're Amazing 1, 2, 3!

By Leslie Kimmelman
Illustrated by Marybeth Nelson
Cover illustration by Tom Brannon

 A GOLDEN BOOK · NEW YORK

This is a picture of Elmo's friend Julia. Elmo and Julia have played together since they were really little. They like to do lots of the same things.

Elmo likes blocks. He builds really tall block
towers. He also likes to knock them down. CRASH!
Julia likes blocks, too. She lines them up in a row.
"Cool wall," Elmo says.

Elmo likes to play with his toy cars
and trucks.

So does Julia. She especially likes spinning the wheels around and around.

Elmo and Julia both like playing games on the tablet. Elmo looks at the screen and giggles.

"Banana begins with the letter Z," he says.

Julia laughs. "No it doesn't!" she says loudly.

Julia goes with Elmo to the playground
because they both LOVE to swing. They even
made up a swinging song. "Swingy swing,
swingity swing," they chant.

Abby arrives at the playground. "Hi, Elmo," says Abby. "Who's your friend?"

"This is Julia. Julia, this is Abby," Elmo says. But Julia doesn't look at Abby.

"Hi!" Abby calls loudly. But Julia doesn't answer.

"Your friend doesn't like me," says Abby sadly.

"Elmo doesn't think that's true," Elmo says. "It's just hard for her to talk when she's swinging."

So Abby waits till Julia is done. "Hi, Julia," she says again. "Can I play with you and Elmo?"

But Julia just looks down. Abby is confused.

"Elmo's daddy told Elmo that Julia has autism," Elmo says. "So she does things a little differently. Sometimes Elmo talks to Julia using fewer words. And sometimes Elmo says the same thing a few times."

"Can I play?" Abby asks Julia. "Can I play?"
But Julia doesn't look at Abby.
 "Oh, and sometimes Elmo waits a long time
for Julia to answer," Elmo adds.
 So Abby and Elmo wait.
 Finally Julia says, "Play with Abby and Elmo."

"Sparkle-tastic!" Abby says. "What should we play?"

Julia says, "Spy?"

"I Spy? I love that game," Abby says. "I spy with my little eye . . . a blue feather."

Julia looks around. She quickly spots something, runs over to it, and comes back with the feather.

She laughs and flaps her hands around and around. Flapping is what Julia does when she's excited.

Elmo jumps up and down, and Abby spins in a pirouette. That's what they do when they're excited.

"You're an expert at I Spy, Julia," Abby says.

Julia starts to sing. She has a pretty voice. She sounds loud and happy.

"Wow. Your singing is really pretty, Julia," says Abby. She joins in, but she forgets the words to the song. She asks Elmo what comes next.

Elmo thinks. "Sorry. Elmo doesn't remember."

But Julia remembers. She remembers the words to song after song. The three new pals sing together for a long time.

"So what should we do next?" asks Elmo.

"Snack!" says Julia. Off to Hooper's Store!

But inside Hooper's Store, Julia seems
scared. She claps her hands over her ears.

"What's the matter?" asks Abby.

"Julia has really good ears," Elmo explains.

"Sometimes she hears noises that Elmo doesn't notice. Like the noise the blender makes. She really doesn't like it!"

"Don't worry, guys," says Alan. "I'll turn the blender off."

Then Julia takes her hands away from her ears.

"Hot cocoa for me!" Abby decides.
"Hot cocoa for Elmo, too," Elmo says.
But now Julia seems worried. She shakes
her head back and forth. "No hot!" she says.

Alan thinks for a minute. "*Cold* chocolate milk for you, Julia," he tells her.

"Thanks!" Elmo and Abby say.

"One, two, three mugs," Julia counts.

"Yeah! And one, two, three friends!" Abby counts, pointing to each of them.

The three friends sip their drinks.
"And one, two, three milk mustaches,"
counts Elmo, giggling.

"We're all amazing, one, two, three!"